For Mazzy, Nonie, and Nancy C. —**M.O.**

For Alma and for Cade. —**B.B.**

Text copyright © 2020 by Micol Ostow
Illustrations copyright © 2020 by Brian Biggs
Published by Roaring Brook Press
Roaring Brook Press is a division of Holtzbrinck Publishing Holdings Limited Partnership
120 Broadway, New York, NY 10271
mackids.com

Library of Congress Cataloging-in-Publication Data is available.
ISBN 978-1-250-30772-9

Our books may be purchased in bulk for promotional, educational, or business use.
Please contact your local bookseller or the Macmillan Corporate and Premium Sales Department at (800) 221-7945 ext. 5442
or by email at MacmillanSpecialMarkets@macmillan.com.

First edition, 2020
Book design by Jen Keenan and Monique Sterling
Printed in China by Toppan Leefung Printing Ltd., Dongguan City, Guangdong Province

1 3 5 7 9 10 8 6 4 2

SULLiVAN,

written by

MiCoL OStoW

illustrated by

Brian Biggs

who is always TOO LOUD

ROARING BROOK PRESS
NEW YORK

This is Sullivan, who is always too loud.

Not just sometimes.
Not just often.

Always.

At home, Mama says:

You're not SUPPOSED to hear THINKING!

Sullivan shouts.
He shouts it *loudly*.

And Ella-baby wakes.
And the dog barks.
And Mr. Jenkins downstairs
raps on their floor—
his ceiling—
with his cane.

(Mr. Jenkins likes quiet
at night.)

Rapping with his cane
means: *Keep it down,
Sullivan.*

Sullivan tries his best.
Mama says, "It's a start."

At school, Ms. Chow says:

Sullivan, it's reading time now.

Sullivan, it's Leah's turn for Share Chair.

Sullivan, Ms. Gonzalez cannot teach percussion with your cymbals crashing away.

Sullivan smashes his cymbals—
loudly—once more. Because *percussion*
means a BOOMING sound.
So Ms. Chow should be proud.

She sends Sullivan to the Peace Place, for thinking.

Quiet.

Sullivan tries to explain to Mama:
"I have loudness. In my body. Bubbling up.
Always.

"And it always has to come out."

He makes a *giant Tarzan jungle*

YELL

Mama says, "It does not have to come out at the grocery store."

All through dinner,

all through bath time,

all through bedtime story,

Sullivan squishes his loudness
down,
down,
down.

But the next morning, it bubbles back up.

Outside, Mr. Jenkins sits on the stoop in his green every-Wednesday suit.

Green like a ferocious dinosaur.

Sullivan is a dinosaur, too.

His loudness
BUBBLES
up
into a

FEROCIOUS

DINO—

OOPS.
Mr. Jenkins frowns.
Frowning means: *Oh, SULLIVAN.*

Mama asks, "Have you tried counting *one, two, three*?"

ONE
TWO
THREE!

Mama sighs.
She says, "It's a start."

At school, Sullivan tries again:

During Center Time, when there are no red blocks.

During Share Chair, when it's Boden's turn.

During Movement, which is for silly jumping.

It's not easy.
But counting squishes the loudness down.

At recess, Boden gives Sullivan a turn with his yellow super-high-bounce ball. Sullivan wants to sing a bouncing song at the tip-top of his lungs:

BOING
BOING
BOING
BOING

But the loudness is squished so deep down
inside that the song won't come.

What if . . .
the loudness is squished inside . . .
*. . .**FOREVER?***

BUT!

THEN!

When it's time to go inside,
everyone lines up—
everyone except . . .

She's far away,
in the tall-grass-*monster* corner of the playground.
She doesn't hear Ms. Chow.

Sullivan feels a
bubble
bubble
BUBBLE
rumble up.

OH NO!

Now is eyes-on-teacher time.
But Sullivan *must*.

Now the tree stump is a
JUNGLE KING PLATFORM!

ONE
TWO
THREE!

His loudness!
It's THERE!

He gives an **ENORMOUS EXTRA-WILD TARZAN JUNGLE YELL!**

Annalise hears!
She comes running!

And Ms. Chow?

She *smiles*!

"Thank you, Sullivan, for choosing the right time for loudness."

Sullivan is
proud,
proud,
proud.

The feeling
bubbles up.

Sullivan tries to
count:
one,
two—

But Ms. Chow just *laughs*.

She says, "It's a start."

And Sullivan laughs, too.